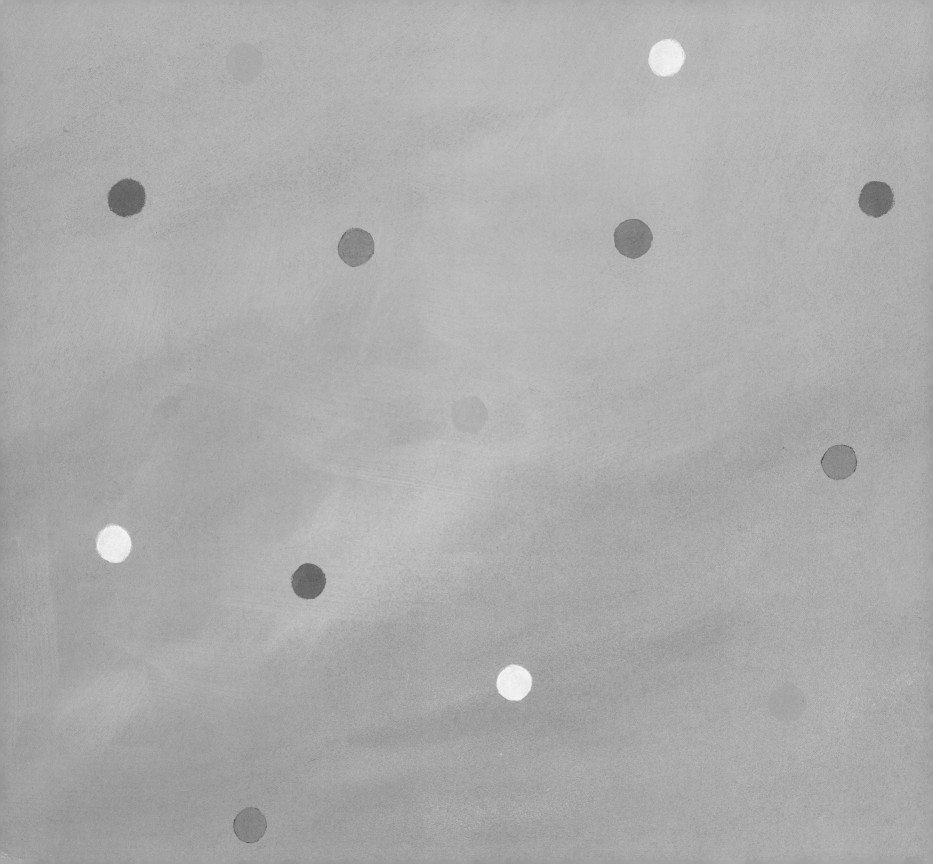

Bear COUNTS

Karma Wilson

Illustrations by
Jane Chapman

Margaret K. McElderry Books • New York London Toronto Sydney New Delhi

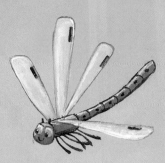

Mouse and Bear share breakfast,
basking in the morning sun.
Bear looks up and points,
and the bear
counts . . .

one!

One sun floating high.

One giant dragonfly.

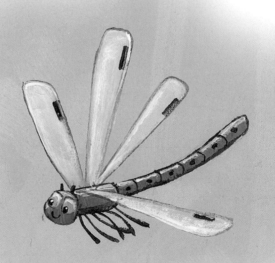

One robin on her nest.
Only ONE berry left!

Numbers, numbers everywhere.
Can you count along with Bear?

1!

Mouse and Bear see Hare,
and Hare calls out, "Howdy do?"
He is holding yummy fruit,
and the bear

counts . . .

two!

Two paws which hold a treat.
Two apples crisp and sweet!

Two stumps for perfect chairs.
Two friends who love to share.

Numbers, numbers everywhere.
Can you count along with Bear?

1,2!

Bear hears funny sounds
coming from an aspen tree.
It is Raven, Owl, and Wren,
and the bear

counts . . .

three!

Three chums who chitter-chat.
Three funny muskrats.

Three clouds above the trees.

Three bumbling bumblebees.

Numbers, numbers everywhere.
Can you count along with Bear?

1,2,3!

Bear cries, "Look, it's Badger,
Mole, and Gopher by the shore!
Badger has his fishin' pole."
And the bear
counts . . .

four!

Four fish splish 'n' splash.

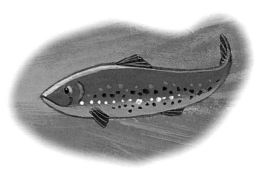

Four geese waddle past.

Four turtles on a log.

Four croaking, hopping frogs!

Numbers, numbers everywhere.
Can you count along with Bear?

1,2,3,4!

Mouse squeaks, "Let's go swimming!"
And in the pond they dive.
The friends float in the pond.
And the bear
counts . . .

five!

Five ducks in the water.

Five lively river otters.

Five lovely lily pads.

Five pinching crawdads.

Numbers, numbers everywhere.
Now YOU can count, just like BEAR!

1!

2!

3!

One, two, three gorgeous kids! Can you count with Karma?
To Sarah, Nathan, David Brian, Atticus Daniel,
and Louisa Belle. All my love!
—K. W.

To Dylan, Jacob, and Bump
—J. C.

THE BEAR BOOKS • MARGARET K. MCELDERRY BOOKS • An imprint of Simon & Schuster Children's Publishing Division • 1230 Avenue of the Americas, New York, New York 10020 • Text copyright © 2015 by Karma Wilson • Illustrations copyright © 2015 by Jane Chapman • All rights reserved, including the right of reproduction in whole or in part in any form. • MARGARET K. MCELDERRY BOOKS is a trademark of Simon & Schuster, Inc. • For information about special discounts for bulk purchases, please contact Simon & Schuster Special Sales at 1-866-506-1949 or business@simonandschuster.com. • The Simon & Schuster Speakers Bureau can bring authors to your live event. For more information or to book an event, contact the Simon & Schuster Speakers Bureau at 1-866-248-3049 or visit our website at www.simonspeakers.com. • Book design by Lauren Rille • The text for this book is set in Adobe Caslon. • The illustrations for this book are rendered in acrylic paint. • Manufactured in China • 0215 SCP • 10 9 8 7 6 5 4 3 2 1 • Library of Congress Cataloging-in-Publication Data • Wilson, Karma. • Bear counts / Karma Wilson ; Illustrations by Jane Chapman. • pages cm • Summary: As friends Bear and Mouse share a day together, Bear counts various objects, from one to five, and the reader is invited to do the same. • ISBN 978-1-4424-8092-6 (hardcover : alk. paper) — ISBN 978-1-4424-8093-3 (ebook) [1. Stories in rhyme. 2. Bears—Fiction. 3. Mice—Fiction. 4. Friendship—Fiction. 5. Counting—Fiction.] I. Chapman, Jane, 1970– illustrator. II. Title. PZ8.3.W6976Baq 2015 • [E]—dc23 • 2014015913

FIRST
EDITION